ס"ד

THE GREAT POTATO PLAN

— *Based on true events* —

Written and Illustrated
by Joy Nelkin Wieder

Hachai
PUBLISHING

Dedicated to Our Darling Children

Jessica and Melissa Katz

❦ ❦ ❦

THE GREAT POTATO PLAN

FIRST EDITION
July 1999 — Tammuz 5759

For my great-grandparents, Nathan and Rose Nelkin, and for their children's
children's children's children — Shira, Seth and Carly Wieder. J.N.W.

Copyright © 1999 by **HACHAI PUBLISHING**
ALL RIGHTS RESERVED

This book, or parts thereof, may not be reproduced, stored, or copied in any
form without written permission from the copyright holder, except by a
reviewer who wishes to quote brief passages in connection with a review
written for inclusion in magazines or newspapers.

Editor: D. L. Rosenfeld
Layout: Spotlight Design
Typesetting: N. Hackner

Library of Congress Catalog Card Number: 99-62137
ISBN # 0-922613-89-3

Hachai Publishing
156 Chester Avenue • Brooklyn, N.Y. 11218
Tel: (718) 633-0100 • Fax: (718) 633-0103
www.hachai.com

Table of Contents

❦ ❦ ❦

❦ ❦ ❦

Meet the family...

 Papa — Noyach Nelkenbaum
He journeyed to America
to make a better life for
his family.

 Mama — Ruchel Nelkenbaum
Her strength kept everyone
hopeful during the long
years of World War I.

 Temela — As the oldest child, she
was the first to join Papa
in America.

 Suri — age 14 - She helped Mama
care for the younger
children while they waited
to leave Poland.

 Simcha — age 13 - As the first born
son, he felt responsible to
be the "man of the house"
until his whole family
could be reunited.

Toba — age 10 - She loved to spend time with her best friend, Hindel. But she had to work hard and help with the Great Potato Plan.

Chana — age 8 - With her freckled nose and wavy auburn hair, she was the "princess" of the family.

Gershon — age 6 - Mama always sent Gershon to Cheder, even when times were tough. He was a model student.

Zisha — age 4 - Born after Papa had left for America, Zisha was Mama's baby that everyone showered with love.

Chapter One

Getting Ready

Simcha pulled an armload of ancient books off the shelf and handed them to his sister, Chana. The children laughed and joked, making the work seem like play. Chana stuffed the books into a wicker trunk.

"Oh, Simcha, can you believe we are finally going to America?" she cried.

"I can't wait to see Papa again!" replied Simcha.

"And Temela," added Suri.

Simcha noticed the loneliness in his big sister's eyes. Suri had cried for weeks when their oldest sister left to join Papa. Suri still missed Temela most of all.

"Yes, and Temela, too," Simcha agreed, mopping the sweat from his face. As the oldest boy, he'd always felt so responsible for the family while his father was in America. At thirteen years old he was the "man" of the house, sturdily built with brown eyes and dark hair. He'd be so relieved when they were all reunited again.

The still air seemed to hang on Simcha like a blanket. "It was just like this the day Papa left Warsaw," he said.

"I remember, but I bet Gershon and Zisha don't," Chana said loud enough for her younger brothers to hear.

Zisha dropped the tablecloth he was folding with Gershon. "I do so!" he exclaimed, hands on hips.

"How could you?" asked Toba, tossing a long, brown braid over her shoulder. "You're only four! You weren't even born when Papa went away."

Toba turned to her best friend, Hindel, who was helping her pack the extra clothes. They both giggled.

"Stop teasing Zishaleh," Suri declared.

"Enough bickering, *kinder*," commanded Mama. "Simcha, help me pack these dishes before Shabbos begins."

Simcha passed the dishes to Mama. Racing against the sun, her hands flew as she wrapped each one in a tattered rag. Suddenly Mama paused, gently stroking a fine china bowl.

"I suppose I should have sold these too, but I just couldn't bear to part with my best Shabbos dishes."

"It's all right, Mama. We have to make Shabbos in America, too."

"You're right, Simcha. It's nice to know not everything changes," Mama said, sighing. She looked around, evaluating their progress.

"Well, that's it for now. We need to leave some dishes for Shabbos dinner." She clapped her hands. "Children, time to wash up! Hindel, you run home and help your mother, now."

"Yes, Mrs. Nelkenbaum. Good-bye, Toba."

"Good-bye, Hindel. Will I see you tomorrow?" asked Toba.

"Yes, of course. I'm so happy there's one day a week when I don't have to sell caps for Papa in the market!"

Simcha turned on the faucet and splashed the cloudy water on his face. The others crowded around the sink, pushing him out of the way.

As he dried off, Simcha took stock of the tiny one-room apartment. It seemed even more cramped with the trunks stacked up against the wall. The bookshelves were bare and the cupboard was all but empty. Otherwise, everything remained the same.

There was the tiled fireplace that served as both oven and furnace. Against

the far wall were two small beds beneath the only window. Zisha and Gershon slept in one bed; Mama in the other. The straw mattresses for Simcha and his sisters were piled on the wooden floor.

In the middle of the room was the scarred oak table that was used for everything from chopping vegetables and eating meals to studying Torah. Tonight the table was set with the good white tablecloth, the silver candlesticks and kiddush cup, and Mama's best dishes.

Mama laid freshly laundered Shabbos clothes on her bed: long black caftans for the boys; beautiful dresses for the girls.

Simcha took off his weekday clothes and slipped into his caftan. The smooth silk felt cool and luxurious as he tied the sash around his waist.

Simcha breathed deeply, filling his nose with the smell of bubbling chicken soup and simmering cholent. All that packing had worked up his appetite.

Eager to begin Shabbos, he snatched off his cap and placed Papa's best yarmulke beneath it. The special yarmulke was black velvet with gold brocade trim. Papa had given it to Simcha, and taken his worn, everyday yarmulke to America.

"Papa's yarmulke sure is big," thought Simcha. "When will it ever fit me?"

Rubbing the soft velvet, Simcha remembered Papa's words: "Since you'll be the man in the family, I'm leaving you my very own Shabbos yarmulke. Take care of Mama and the children while I'm gone."

Eighteen minutes before sunset, Mama signaled the children to gather around her. Simcha looked at the shining faces of his family. Mama, round and soft, but with an inner strength of steel, glowed with the peace of Shabbos. Even her care-worn face seemed radiant.

Suri stood by Mama. At fourteen, she had grown into an elegant young lady. Her long, brunette hair was softly pulled back from her slender face, and she looked even more beautiful in her Shabbos finest.

Toba, her brown hair neatly brushed and tied with ribbons, helped eight-year-old Chana put a white candle into her own little candlestick.

"That's not how you do it; watch me," ordered Toba.

Chana wrinkled her freckled nose and shook her wavy, auburn hair. "Just because you're ten, doesn't mean you can tell me what to do."

"Girls, no fighting on Shabbos," Suri reminded them.

Standing next to Simcha were the two littlest ones, Gershon, six, and Zisha, four. Gershon, thin and knobby-kneed in his short pants, was the scholar in the house. He studied hard and did well at cheder.

Zisha, the baby, was constantly spoiled by everyone, especially Mama. Simcha suspected that she felt sorry for him.

Born two months after Papa had left for America, Zisha was the only one in the family who had never seen their father. Now, four years later, he was a fair-haired, rosy-cheeked boy with large brown eyes that could melt Simcha's heart.

Suri, Toba and Chana lit their own, small candles, and Mama lit her tall white ones. Bringing the holy light of Shabbos into their hearts, Mama and the girls slowly circled their flickering candles with cupped hands. Together, they raised their hands to their eyes and gently swayed back and forth, whispering the special brochah.

After the candles were lit, Simcha, Gershon and Zisha walked to shul. Simcha held Zisha's hand, as Papa would have done. Their shul wasn't fancy, like the huge Tzomackie Synagogue, with its towering columns and domed roof. They couldn't afford anything like that.

Theirs was a one-room synagogue in the basement of the building down the street. A small aron kodesh stood in front of five rows of hard wooden benches. As long as there were at least ten men, a minyan, they could welcome the Shabbos Queen.

Simcha and his brothers returned home after dark. Simcha knew exactly what Mama would say — it was the same every Friday night.

"Since Papa isn't here, Simcha will make kiddush."

Everyone gathered around the table in their usual places. Papa's seat at the head of the table remained empty. Simcha

wore Papa's velvet yarmulke and made kiddush in his place, but he couldn't sit in Papa's chair. That would be disrespectful.

Simcha held the kiddush cup high while blessing the wine. He took a sip and passed it to Mama. She took a taste and passed the becher for each child to savor the sweetness of Shabbos.

Before starting the meal, they all washed their hands by pouring water over them three times and saying the brochah. Silently, Simcha removed the challah cover, revealing two smooth, braided loaves of bread. He made a small cut with the challah knife on one of the loaves.

Then he held them together and said Hamotzi. After he passed a slice to each person, everyone broke off a piece from the bread, dipped it in salt and repeated the brochah.

Then the Shabbos meal began. Mama brought out gefilte fish and chicken soup, followed by roasted chicken, tzimmes and a mouth-watering potato kugel.

"You've outdone yourself this time, Mama. The kugel is delicious," Simcha exclaimed.

"And the chicken is so tender, it falls off the bone," Suri said.

Unable to contain his excitement, Zisha announced, "I can't wait to go to America!"

"Me, too," Chana agreed, pushing back a loose strand of auburn hair.

"But I'll be sad to leave my friends, especially Hindel," said Toba.

"Yes, but we'll be with Papa and Temela!" Gershon cried.

After dinner, the family sang Zmiros

and the Birchas Hamazon. Soon there was a knock on the door. It was the building superintendent.

"Good evening, Mr. Grabowski," said Mama.

"Good Sabbath to you, Mrs. Nelkenbaum. Are you ready for me to turn off the lamps?"

"Yes, thank you," Mama answered.

Because lighting or extinguishing fire during Shabbos is forbidden, Mr. Grabowski, who was not Jewish, turned out the lights of all the Jewish families in his building each Friday night.

In the cozy darkness, Simcha and his family said Shema and stumbled into bed. Their stomachs were full of Shabbos delicacies, their dreams filled with America . . . and Papa.

Chapter Two

Bad News

The following Sunday was Tishah B'Av, a day as somber and mournful as Shabbos was peaceful and joyous. As a sign of mourning, Simcha and his family sat on the hard floor.

"You see, *kinder*," explained Mama, "Ever since the destruction of the Beis Hamikdosh, our holy Temple in Yerushalayim, Jews have wandered the earth, always strangers in a strange land."

"Is Papa a stranger in America?" asked Zisha.

Mama thought for a moment. "Well, yes —until the Beis Hamikdosh is rebuilt, and we have our own land again, we are always strangers. But America is different from any place we've ever been. There, people are free to live the way they like without fear. That's why Papa is in America making a new home for us."

Simcha's heart soared. Wouldn't it be wonderful to finally feel at home? In Poland, Jews were treated harshly, herded into ghettos and unable to own land.

He thought about poor Uncle Moishe and his family, who lost their home and belongings in a bloody pogrom. Yes, the sooner they got out of Poland, the better.

"Gershon, read to us," said Mama.

Gershon picked up Eichah, the Book of Lamentations, its leather cover worn and faded. His voice cracked, as he read, "Judah is gone into exile because of affliction, and because of great servitude; She lives among the nations, She finds no rest..."

Simcha tried to listen, but found it hard to focus. Since he had his Bar Mitzvah, he must fast during Tishah B'Av. He had not eaten since yesterday evening, and he felt dizzy. His head was so light, he thought it might float away.

Suddenly the door burst open, startling everyone. Uncle Yankel ran in. He grabbed Simcha by the arms, pulling the boy to his feet.

"Have you heard? Have you heard?" Uncle Yankel shouted.

"Calm down," Mama commanded.

"Have we heard what?" asked Simcha.

"The Germans have declared war against Russia," Yankel panted. "As part of the Russian Empire, Poland will be mixed up in it, too!"

"Oy vey!" Mama cried, clutching her

shawl. "Has the whole world gone crazy?"

"Don't worry, Mama!" Suri exclaimed. "In two days, with Hashem's help, we leave for America. The war won't touch us!"

"With Germany and Russia at war, all the passenger ships may be stuck here," Mama moaned.

The gloomy atmosphere grew even heavier. Simcha's heart pounded. What if they weren't able to leave now? They might never see Papa again. And what if he were forced to sign up for the Russian army — he might never see anyone again!

The Tzar who ruled Russia might keep him in the army so long that he'd forget how to be Jewish. Besides, the Cossacks made the Jewish boys do all the dangerous work. Not a day went by without Mama warning him, "Beware of the Cossacks!"

Simcha sat back down on the floor and buried his face in his hands.

Two days, just two more days. Would he be on a ship to America and Papa, or would he be facing the dangers of war?

* * *

The following day, Uncle Yankel returned with more bad news for Mama.

"The borders are closed, Ruchel. You can't leave Poland, and even if you could, no passenger ships are allowed to sail."

Simcha swallowed hard. It felt as if a lump of coal were stuck in his throat. Chana began to cry.

Uncle Yankel looked at her and said softly, "Don't worry, it won't last long. The Germans have cannons that can blast a hundred Cossacks at a time!"

For the last one hundred and twenty

years, Poland had been under Russian control. During that time, the tzars had done everything they could to make the Jews suffer.

Now, Poland was once again the battleground between two giants, Russia and Germany. Simcha and his family hoped the Germans would finally force Russia out of Poland once and for all.

Mama sighed. "We may as well unpack and get the household back in order."

This time there was no laughing or joking. Simcha's hands felt like lead weights as he unloaded the worn, old books, the clothing and family photos they had packed for their trip to America. His spirits sank lower and lower with each article he emptied from the trunk.

At first, they believed Uncle Yankel's

prediction for a quick victory as the Germans forced Russia to retreat. Within months their hopes sank when the Yiddish newspapers reported Russian advances into Galicia.

Week after week, deadly accounts of pogroms in different towns were in the news. Russia blamed the Jews for their own swift defeats, accusing them of spying for the Germans.

"I hope the Germans come to Warsaw," said Toba.

"And get rid of those terrible Cossacks," added Gershon.

"That would be a miracle," agreed Simcha.

Chapter Three

War Rations

To his dismay, Simcha watched the bulge of coins in Mama's handkerchief, her *knippl*, shrink each time she went to market or paid the rent. The money Papa had sent before the war was running out.

Papa's last letter arrived opened, the money stolen.

One morning, Mama rummaged deeply into her petticoat pocket. She pulled out her *knippl* and untied the knot, revealing the last few coins. She handed them to Simcha.

"Go to market and buy three loaves of bread for Shabbos. Beware of the Cossacks!"

Simcha quietly asked, "Mama, when will we see Papa again?"

"Hashem alone knows," Mama answered. "We can only pray for this war to end quickly."

Simcha crossed the courtyard of 65 Stawki Street, dodging clumps of children playing war games, hide-and-seek and hopscotch. He opened the gate and entered the stream of people on the crowded avenue.

City noises bombarded him: horse-drawn droshkies rumbling over the cobblestones; women hawking their wares and shopkeepers haggling with their customers.

He crossed over Niska Street, heading toward the outskirts of Warsaw's Jewish Quarter. When he reached The Square of the Iron Gates, the scents and sounds of the market place swirled around him.

Rotting vegetables mingled with chicken droppings, bearded Jews in long, black coats bargained with Polish peasants in brightly embroidered sheepskin jackets. Peddlers jostled their pushcarts, calling out their wares.

"Used pots, like new!"

"Best fish here!"

"Rags, rags for sale!"

Simcha took his place in the long bread line. Supplies had run low. Simcha had even heard of shopkeepers hoarding goods to raise prices.

In either case, food was rationed, and the lines formed earlier and earlier each day; sometimes even overnight. Simcha slowly inched forward, watching the sun sink lower and lower in the sky.

"I'll be late for Shabbos," worried Simcha.

By the time Simcha trudged home on frozen feet, long shadows fell across the courtyard of his building. The gate creaked as it swung open.

Simcha hurried across the cobblestones, pinching his nose past the reeking outhouse. It was a filthy, rat-

infested pit; the only bathroom for more than three hundred families.

He stopped just inside the entryway, adjusting to the murky gloom. Peeling plaster curled from the walls and garbage was strewn everywhere. Smoke from the kerosene lamps stung Simcha's eyes and threw dancing shadows on the walls.

Shivers ran up his spine as he imagined bloodthirsty Cossacks hiding in the darkness. He dashed up the stairs to the third floor landing.

Simcha bolted through the door, slamming it quickly behind him. Mama grabbed him and cried, "My boy! What took you so long? Are you all right?"

"I'm fine, Mama," Simcha tried to assure her, still shaking and breathless. "But they only gave me two loaves of bread. War rations."

"Not to worry, Simcha. He Who gave us teeth will give us bread. Now go clean up for Shabbos — and hurry!"

Simcha sprinted to the sink. He washed and scrubbed until his skin glowed. He quickly put on his Shabbos caftan and Papa's velvet yarmulke.

Mama called, "Simcha! It's time to light the candles."

In the glow of the flames, Simcha's fears subsided. The calm of Shabbos filled his soul and eased his mind.

When the boys returned from shul, the Shabbos rituals proceeded as always. But when Simcha removed the cover from the bread, there were no golden brown challos underneath — only the two loaves of hard bread he had bought at the market. After making the brochah, he quartered each loaf, giving each person a hunk of bread.

Mama looked at the expectant faces around the table. "I'm sorry, *kinder*, I wish I had more."

Simcha looked into Mama's round face. The wide-set brown eyes and thin, chiseled mouth seldom smiled, but Simcha detected a grimness he hadn't noticed before. The dark circles under her eyes worried him.

Only a few months ago, their Shabbos table had looked like a feast set for a king. Now, Simcha took a small bite of his dry bread, chewing slowly to make it last as long as possible.

He closed his eyes and imagined hot soup with long, slippery noodles sliding down his throat. "But we do have more, Mama. This chicken soup is delicious!"

He looked around the table, silently encouraging the others to join the game.

Toba nibbled her bread. "This brisket is the best I've ever eaten." Everyone nodded in agreement.

Even the youngest, Zisha, played along. He gnawed at his crust of bread and exclaimed, "Mmmm, good kasha!"

"Yes," said Gershon. "I've never tasted a better potato kugel in my life!"

Mama smiled one of her rare smiles.

"My brave, brave children," she said softly.

Simcha grinned at his brothers and sisters. His stomach was empty, but his heart was full of love.

* * *

The next evening, when three stars were visible in the wedge of sky above the courtyard, Mama and the children said goodbye to Shabbos. They lit the braided havdallah candle and passed the spice box, breathing deeply of the pungent besomim.

Usually full to overflowing, the kiddush cup held only a splash of wine. Simcha made the blessing and took a tiny sip. He examined his fingernails in the candle light then quenched the candle in the remaining wine.

That night Simcha lay awake,

listening to the rumbling of his empty stomach. He heard noises at the table and went over to investigate.

"Mama, you're crying!"

"No, no, it's just these onions," Mama protested. "They always make my eyes water." She jabbed the knife into an onion. "I was saving these for breakfast but look at all these blemishes! I'll be lucky to save half an onion apiece."

Simcha knew it wasn't the onions making Mama cry. "I sure miss Papa," he said.

"So do I," Mama whispered, laying down the knife. Simcha took his mother's hands. Tears flowed silently down her cheeks. "I also miss my Temela. She's growing into a young woman without me."

Simcha missed his big sister, too. She

could always make him laugh, even during hard times.

Mama wiped her eyes. "It's late. Time for you to go to bed. Don't worry, Simcha, we'll be all right."

"You know," said Simcha, "we could always ask Uncle Yankel for a loan."

"No!" Mama said vehemently.

"He already brings us a few things we need, like wine for Shabbos," Simcha argued.

"That's different. I won't accept charity, even from my own brother."

"But he's better off than we are and can well afford to help us," Simcha pressed.

"It's out of the question," Mama said. "Now, don't you worry anymore. I'll think of something to keep us going."

Reluctantly Simcha returned to bed, but he couldn't fall asleep. Papa's last words echoed in his mind:

"Take care of Mama and the children while I'm gone."

But how could he feed them all? Simcha reached for Papa's yarmulke and put it on in the darkness. The others would laugh if they knew, but Simcha sometimes wore it when he had a difficult problem to solve....or when he felt afraid.

Perhaps he could become an apprentice and learn a trade — yet, there were many unemployed tradesmen these days. Maybe he could travel to the country and find work on a farm — but it was winter and none of the peasants needed help.

Still, Simcha imagined himself plowing the fields; shearing the sheep; hoeing the potatoes. Yum, how he loved

potatoes, especially Mama's potato kugel. He could almost taste the brown, crunchy crust with the soft potato and onion mixture hiding underneath. His mouth watered and his stomach grumbled even louder. This was no good, it only made him hungrier.

He wiggled further under the covers, trying to get warm. Mama couldn't afford to heat the apartment, and Simcha was shivering.

The straw in the mattress poked him in the knee. When he rolled over, it stabbed him in the back.

Eventually, he fell into a troubled sleep. In his dreams, starved, ragged children begged him for food, but he had nothing to give them. He tried to run away but could not escape their pleading eyes.

Chapter Four
Potato Kugel

Simcha was the first to arise the next morning. He washed negel vasser and tried to dress quickly, but his stiff, frozen fingers pulled clumsily at his heavy trousers.

His breath froze in white puffs as he labored to button his jacket. The early morning light shone through the frost on the window, transforming it into an intricate panel of frozen lace.

After davening, Simcha opened the cupboard in search of a small morsel of food. All he found were the few bruised onions Mama had tried to save. Grimly, he headed for the front door.

"Where are you going so early, Simcha?" Mama called from her bed. "It's freezing cold!" She and the children often stayed in bed until noon to keep warm.

"I'm going to find a job."

"Dress warmly," Mama replied. "Use Suri's kerchief for a scarf. And beware of the Cossacks!"

Wrapping the kerchief around his neck, Simcha ran through the biting cold to the market. He had never seen the city so quiet. All he heard was the crunching of new fallen snow under his boots.

A few of the vendors were setting up their stalls. Reb Nutah and his son, Ephraim, were unloading cans of milk and cheese from his cart. Their horse stamped impatiently and shook his head.

"Easy, boy," called Reb Nutah.

Just as Ephraim was reaching for the next milk jug, a rat ran under the cart. The horse stepped on the rat's tail. The rat turned and dug its long, yellow teeth into the horse's leg.

"Watch out!" shouted Simcha, but it was too late. The horse reared, sending the rat, the cart, Ephraim and the milk jugs flying. Ephraim landed with a thud under a

pile of metal cans. The rat scurried away, but Ephraim did not move.

Simcha rushed to help Reb Nutah pull the containers off his son. Ephraim moaned. Reb Nutah's wife ran from the store, screaming.

"I think his arm is broken," Reb Nutah announced.

"Oy gevald! Take him to the doctor and get it set," ordered his wife.

"But who will unload the goods and set up the store?"

"I can help," said Simcha, stepping forward. "I'm small, but I'm strong." Simcha took after his mother's side, short and sturdy.

Reb Nutah's wife squinted at him. "All right, you'll do. But no loafing."

"Yes, ma'am."

"You can start by loading those cans in the back."

Simcha worked hard all morning. By the time Reb Nutah and Ephraim returned, Simcha had stripped off his scarf and jacket and was even beginning to sweat.

Reb Nutah patted his head. "You're a good boy, Simcha. Your father would be very proud." Then he dug into his pocket and pulled out three coins.

Simcha beamed. "Thank you, Reb Nutah, thank you!" He felt like the richest man in the world; he felt like a king. Simcha seized the money in a tight fist and shook it at the sky, as if to say, "Thank you, Hashem!"

Simcha strolled through the market, looking over the goods with disdain. The women who sold fruit and vegetables had little to offer, and the supplies in the stores were low. Now that he finally had some money, there was very little to buy.

"Potatoes today, boychick?" asked a wizened, old peasant woman. Simcha went over to examine her produce.

The apples were bruised and rotten but the potatoes were firm and brown. He did so love Mama's potato kugel. Then an idea began to form in his mind.

"How much for the whole sack?"

"One bag, one zyloty."

"One zyloty! That's robbery!" Simcha was well versed in the art of bargaining. Peasants expected customers to negotiate for the best price.

"Are you a peddler or a thief? I'll give you twenty groschen," he countered.

"Twenty groschen! Are you trying to steal these potatoes from me? Seventy five and not a groschen less."

"Thirty."

"Sixty."

Simcha threw up his hands. "You're taking food out of the mouths of my family." He turned to walk away.

The old woman called out to him. "All right, fifty groschen."

"Forty and you've got a deal."

The old woman nodded. It was almost

mid-day, and there were few customers. Simcha counted out forty groschen into her gnarled hand, and she offered him the sack of potatoes. He hugged it to his chest as if it were a sack of gold.

When Simcha returned home, everyone was trying to keep warm in bed. He called to Mama and whispered in her ear. She nodded then swung her legs over the side. Simcha gently grasped her arm and helped her stand up.

"Simcha, get some coal and start the fire," Mama ordered. "Suri, peel the potatoes. Toba and Chana, you grate them."

Soon the room was warm and filled with a tantalizing smell, pulling Zisha from his snug bed.

"Yum, potato kugel," he said, reaching for a piece.

"This isn't for you," Simcha cried, pushing his small hand away. Zisha looked at Simcha with his big brown eyes; a small tear ran down his cheek. Simcha softened.

"I'm bringing these to the market," he explained.

"It's all right if he has just one," said Mama, handing Zisha a piece. "Besides, it's getting late. You can't sell all this today."

"He's so spoiled," Toba complained, twirling her long braid.

"No, he's not," Mama corrected. "He's my baby. Besides, I'm saving a piece for each of you."

Mama smiled at Zisha while he licked his fingers clean. She removed several pieces then handed the large, tin pan to Simcha.

"Don't take less than two groschen a piece!"

On the way back to the Iron Gate, Simcha passed a mother and child in rags. The woman stopped him, begging, "Please, boy, just a small taste for my son?"

"But I must sell these to feed my own family," explained Simcha.

He looked at the scrawny child and remembered his nightmare. Simcha passed the boy a small piece and whispered, "Meet me here tomorrow, and I'll see what I can do."

Once at the market, Simcha stood quietly holding the tin tray. Shyly, he watched the vendors calling out to their customers. Could he really do that?

Suddenly, he heard a familiar voice. "Caps here, caps for sale!" His sister's friend, Hindel, was already hard at work for her family.

Simcha lifted his chin, determined to sell every last piece of kugel. After all, if tiny Hindel could sell her father's caps, surely he could sell Mama's kugel.

Simcha mingled with the crowd, crying out, "Kugel for sale! Fresh, hot kugel!" It wasn't so hard once he got started. The smell of the delicious treat helped, too. Who could resist a hot piece of potato kugel on a freezing cold day?

Simcha walked up and down the bread lines until the pan was empty. Then took his place at the end of the line.

After buying his ration of bread, he still had enough money for tomorrow's supply of potatoes. The Great Potato Plan was a success!

Chapter Five

Cossacks

That night, Simcha told his mother about the beggar woman and her child. "There must be something we can do, even though we don't have much to eat ourselves."

"Your Papa always told us that giving tzedakah is a mitzvah," said Mama. "I think Papa would want us to help."

She paused for a moment and said, "Perhaps we can save the potato peelings for that poor family. At least they will not starve."

The next morning, Simcha scraped the potato peelings into a sack and brought it with him. The woman and her child were waiting for him.

"It's the best I can do," said Simcha, handing her the sack.

The woman smiled. "Thank you, you're very kind. I couldn't bear it if my little Shmuel..." She looked away, hiding her tears. Her child sniffed and rubbed his nose.

"I'll bring you whatever I can," Simcha said softly. "I know how it feels to be hungry."

Just as Simcha arrived at the Iron Gate, five Russian Cossacks stormed into the market on horseback. The women screamed and scattered in confusion. He saw Hindel gather her caps in her apron and run. Simcha dashed into an alley and hid behind a large crate.

Peering around the side, he stifled a cry as he watched a soldier grab an old man's beard and slice it off with his sword.

The Cossacks knew this was a special shame since the Jews never shaved their long, full beards.

Two more Cossacks came upon a young student absorbed in a book. They swooped down, plucked him off his feet and galloped away, leaving only the book behind.

Simcha pitied him. The poor fellow would be forced to fight in the Russian army without a chance to say goodbye to his family.

"What if that happened to me?" worried Simcha. "Who would take care of everyone?"

The last two Cossacks dismounted and strode into the drygoods store. Soon they returned, their arms filled with merchandise. The shopkeeper ran after them shouting, "Wait, you did not pay!"

One of the Cossacks whirled around, pointing his gun at the shopkeeper's chest. "We are the Russian Army! You must do your duty to the Tzar. Or don't you Jews love the Tzar?"

The shopkeeper grinned nervously. "Oh, yes. We love the Tzar. Take it. Take all you need!"

The Cossacks laughed and galloped away. The shopkeeper was so frightened, he fainted on the spot.

Shaking his head, Simcha tried to clear away the horrifying images. Then his fear turned to anger.

"What a coward I was — hiding like a little child! Papa would be so ashamed." Simcha vowed never to hide again. Next time he would be ready for those bullies.

* * *

As winter melted into spring, and spring blossomed into summer, Mama and the girls grated potatoes until their fingers bled. Every weekday, Simcha sold kugel on the streets of Warsaw alongside the other peddlers.

At night, with Papa's yarmulke on his head, he planned. Simcha thought of many ideas to protect his family from the Cossacks, but nothing seemed right.

"I'll just have to see what happens when the time comes," he thought.

Late one night, Simcha was awakened by loud, drunken voices. He crept to the window. Simcha spied two dark shapes in the courtyard below. Cossacks!

Their brass buttons shimmered in the moonlight. Their tall, black boots scuffled across the courtyard as they

staggered into the adjoining building. Simcha heard the Cossacks banging on doors.

"What do they want?" Mama whispered in the darkness. "If **they**'ve come to rob us, they'll find very little."

"I've seen what these bullies can do," Simcha replied. "They're drunk and they're dangerous. They might even take one of us away to the army." Mama gave a muffled cry and hugged Zisha close to her.

Dressing quickly, Simcha decided what he must do. "Mama, put the little ones under the bed. Suri, help me carry these potatoes."

"Why?" asked Suri. Simcha whispered something in her ear.

"You can't do that," Suri hissed.

"I've got to do something!" Simcha retorted. He turned to Mama. "Don't worry, I'll be fine."

"Don't worry? You're only a boy! You can't take on the Russian army."

"Without Papa, I must protect the family. The Cossacks could come here next," he said firmly.

Suri's eyes were wide with fear as she and Simcha struggled to haul the potatoes down to the deserted courtyard. Twice they stopped on the stairs, straining to hear voices or footsteps in the darkness.

At last they reached the courtyard and put down the heavy sacks. Simcha took a deep breath, trying to loosen the tight, trembly feeling in his stomach.

"Suri," he whispered fiercely. "Go upstairs and keep the others calm. They must not make any noise."

"I can't leave you here by yourself!"

"You can, and you will. Now go!"

Suri peered into her brother's determined face, then silently turned away. She sprinted toward the darkened entryway. Simcha hoped that she'd make it safely to their apartment.

Waiting in the shadows, the pounding of his heart filled his ears. Softly, he whispered, "Please, Hashem, just as You delivered my ancestors from the cruel Egyptians, save me now from the hands of the Cossacks."

Suddenly two tall, dark shapes loomed in front of him.

Simcha jumped up, clutching a sack. He threw a large potato as hard as he could.

"Oof!" The first Cossack went down, doubled over in pain. A pair of silver candlesticks he had taken from some other family clattered to the ground.

"Yahoo!" Simcha shouted, wildly flinging potatoes. The second Cossack still lurched toward him through the barrage. In a matter of minutes, nothing was left but two empty sacks.

Thinking quickly, Simcha ran up

behind the Cossack and threw one of the sacks over the soldier's head.

"*Pitsh, patsh*, can't catch me," Simcha taunted. He slipped through the gate. He had to lure those bullies away.

"Hey, grab him!" came a muffled shout.

Simcha turned. The large, clumsy Cossack wrestled with the potato sack. The other one rushed toward him!

Simcha bolted down Stawki Street. Swerving down an alley, he headed for the market. As he raced by the bakery, Simcha stumbled and fell. A sharp pain shot up his leg and he stifled a scream. The pounding of heavy boots grew louder and louder.

"There he is!" one of the soldiers called.

In spite of his injury, Simcha shot up like an arrow and into the shadow of a vendor's cart. Through the spokes, he spied a sewer drain a few yards away. Simcha sprang to the drain, pulling frantically at the grate.

A heavy hand grabbed his shoulder. Desperately, he yanked on the bars. Between the fear pumping through his veins and the Cossack pulling his jacket, the heavy grate popped open.

Simcha fell hard against the Cossack;

they both tumbled to the ground. The Cossack swore and tightened his grip on Simcha's collar. Then Simcha squirmed out of his jacket, leaving it in the Cossack's hand!

Simcha leaped to the drain and paused at the edge of the gaping, black hole. Checking behind, the boy watched the tall soldier offer a hand to his fallen comrade. They'd soon be after him again!

Simcha plugged his nose and jumped into the darkness of the drain, bracing himself for the fall. He dropped about twenty feet into the sewer waters of the main Kanal.

The impact sent more pain up his bad leg. His scream bounced off the slimy, brick walls and echoed down the dark tunnel.

The stench was so foul, his stomach

jumped into his throat. He swallowed hard. There was no time to get sick.

Hearing curses from above, Simcha forced his body to move. Moonlight streaming through the opening gave him some sense of his surroundings. Feeling along the wall, he sloshed through the knee-high muck.

When he was several yards down the Kanal, he heard a splash and a grunt then another splash and a curse. Simcha scrambled as fast as he could through the swiftly running sewage.

"You can't run forever, Jew boy."

"When we catch you, you'll never see your family again!"

The Cossacks' heavy voices swept down the Kanal, sending a chill of fear through his body. He could not outrun trained soldiers in this sludge.

"Well, if I can't outrun them, I'll have to outsmart them," thought Simcha.

Just then his hand came to an opening in the Kanal wall. A drainpipe! Simcha pulled himself up, crawling through the narrow drain.

His heart raced faster than his hands and knees could shuffle. The filthy water lapped against his chin. He clamped his mouth shut.

The Cossacks passed the drain, cursing and calling to him. Simcha froze. When he could no longer hear voices, he collapsed against the curved wall.

Simcha couldn't move. Should he backtrack or go forward? He had no idea where the drain would lead.

"Best to move on," Simcha decided. "Just in case those beasts come back."

Suddenly, Simcha was aware of the pain in his leg. He continued forward in a limping crawl. After what seemed like hours, he felt a rush of air.

I must be coming to the end. Boruch Hashem!

A few minutes later, he reached the end of the drain and pulled himself out into another wide tunnel. This time the sewer water was up to his chest.

The tide must be rising. I've got to get to higher ground.

He scanned the Kanal. The moon's pale light through the drains cast silvery pools on the dark water. Simcha noticed a ledge higher up on the Kanal wall.

He grabbed hold of the edge. His foot slipped. He rested and tried again. This time Simcha got his knee over the top. He pulled himself up and collapsed.

Shivering and soaked to the skin, Simcha curled up and hugged his knees, trying to stay warm. He heard a tiny scuffling sound and saw a small shadow scamper across his boot.

"Even the sewer rats know when to find dry land," Simcha mumbled, but he was glad for the company. It was strangely reassuring to know that he wasn't alone in this dark, damp underworld — even if his only companion was a sewer rat.

Simcha closed his eyes, dreaming of the comforts of home. He thought of his bed with the lumpy, straw mattress and rough blanket. At that moment, it would feel like heaven on earth.

He imagined himself sitting at the kitchen table, sipping a cup of hot tea; Mama teaching Zisha his Aleph-Bais next to him; the others chasing one another around the table, their laughter joyous and free.

Chapter Six

Simcha the Brave

When Simcha opened his eyes, the first streaks of dawn were filtering through the drain covers. He had spent the entire night in the sewer! He tumbled off the ledge stiff with cold.

His leg throbbed, but it was worth the pain if Mama and the children were safe. Simcha hoped that the Cossacks had not gone back to Stawki Street during the night.

Simcha staggered through the sewage. It was knee-high again. He had no idea where he was, but he had to find a way to get out.

After following the current for awhile, he saw a ladder leading up to a manhole. His arms and legs ached, but he pulled himself up each rung. The cover was too heavy. He couldn't lift it. He hooked his arm around the top rung to rest.

"I've got to get out of here," he whispered.

Using the ladder as a brace, Simcha pressed his shoulder against the cover. He pushed and strained until he felt his neck muscles bulge. It moved ever so slightly.

Simcha could see light and breathe fresh air. He filled his lungs and felt a surge of energy. He pushed again, even harder. The cover opened, scraping against the street.

Simcha crawled out of the sewer. He stood up slowly, dripping mud and slime. Dazed and disoriented in the morning light, Simcha tried to recover his bearings.

There was the tailor's shop, and the Kosher butcher. Simcha couldn't believe his eyes! He thought he had traveled for miles through the Kanal. In fact, he was only a few blocks from where he had jumped in.

The city's early risers stared at him in disbelief. Reb Nutah and his son ran over. Hindel's eyes widened in surprise. Leah, the tailor's wife, peered into his face.

"Simcha is that you? What happened?"

"I tried to keep the Cossacks away from my family, and they followed me right into the sewer!"

Leah waved her hand in front of her nose. "You're covered with filth! What will your mother say?"

Mama! Oy, would he catch it when he got home. "I've got to go now."

Simcha limped home as fast as he could. He was relieved to see everyone unharmed and the apartment intact. Then he saw Mama's face. Her eyes were red and her clothes were rumpled. She must have stayed up all night.

"Simcha Bunim Nelkenbaum, look at you!" Mama said. "You're soaking wet, and your jacket's missing — where have you been?"

"I spent the night in the Kanal," answered Simcha. "I had to lead those Cossacks away from here. They chased me through the market and jumped right after me into the sewer!"

"When Suri came back without you, I..."

Simcha braced himself. Mama was beyond angry. To his surprise, she gathered him in her strong arms. "We were sick with worry!"

Mama released Simcha, a smear of mud on her cheek. For the second time in his life, Simcha saw tears in Mama's eyes. This time, it couldn't be onions.

"Now get out of those dirty clothes," she commanded.

After Simcha cleaned himself up, his brothers and sisters sat him in a chair.

They danced around him, as if he were a bridegroom at a wedding.

"Hooray for Simcha!"

"Hooray for Simcha the Brave!"

As they twirled and danced, Mama clapped her hands, and Simcha laughed until his cheeks hurt.

*　*　*

The next morning, Simcha awoke shivering. He was freezing cold and burning hot at the same time. Mama pressed her hand to his forehead.

"You're not going anywhere today." Then she turned to Gershon and said, "You'd better get ready for cheder."

"Yes, Mama," said Gershon, pulling on his jacket and gathering his books.

Simcha had to muster all of his strength to put on his tefillin and daven. Then he dozed while the aroma of baking kugel drifted in and out of his awareness. He heard Mama say, "Suri, you're going to market today. Simcha needs his rest."

"Yes, Mama," said Suri, picking up the steaming tray. Chana and Zisha raced to the door, arguing about who should open it.

"Will one of you please open the door," said Suri, annoyed. "This is heavy."

"Chana, let Zisha open the door," Mama called.

"It's not fair. He always gets to do everything," cried Chana.

Simcha smiled to himself, rolled over, and was instantly asleep.

* * *

Simcha opened his eyes and blinked. The late afternoon sun spilled through the lone window, and he realized that he had slept through most of the day.

"Hello, sleepyhead," said Toba. "Mama made kreplach to help you feel better."

Simcha sat up while Toba propped the pillow behind him. Chana walked carefully to Mama's bed, holding a

steaming bowl of chicken soup with kreplach.

Ever since Simcha started selling Mama's kugel, they had managed to make enough profit to buy their basic needs. On a rare occasion, Mama bought fish or chicken, but she usually saved it for Shabbos. Simcha knew Mama must really be worried about him if she made chicken soup on a regular weekday.

"That smells wonderful," said Simcha, breathing in the rich aroma. He dipped the spoon in the bowl then blew across it. He closed his eyes, made the brochah and sipped the golden liquid.

"Ahhhh...that makes me warm from the inside out!"

At twilight, the door flew open and Suri burst into the tiny apartment. "Simcha, you were the talk of the marketplace! The tailor's wife was telling everyone about your bravery."

Simcha smiled, but felt a little uneasy. What if those two Cossacks got wind of such gossip? They wouldn't like being the joke of the entire Jewish Quarter.

Simcha stayed home another day, even though he was feeling better. He kept Papa's yarmulke under his pillow, hoping some of his father's courage would rub off on him.

By the third day, he knew he couldn't hide in bed any longer. Mama needed Suri's help at home. He'd have to go to market, but he was afraid those Cossacks were looking for him.

Simcha stood up too quickly, making his head swim. He grabbed the bed frame until the dizziness cleared. With shaking hands, he got dressed, secretly placing Papa's yarmulke under his cap.

"Are you sure you're strong enough to go to market today?" asked Mama.

"Yes, Mama. I'm fine."

"How's your leg?"

"Boruch Hashem, much better, Mama."

Out on the street, Simcha walked slowly, dragging his feet and looking over his shoulder. He expected the two Cossacks to reach out and grab him at every turn.

When he finally arrived at The Square of the Iron Gates, the marketplace was buzzing.

"There he is!" said Mendel the blacksmith. "Our very own hero."

"Yes, Simcha, you chased them clear out of town," said Reb Nutah, laughing.

"What do you mean?" asked Simcha.

Reb Nutah's son, Ephraim, answered, "Haven't you heard the news? The German soldiers are here. They pushed the Cossacks clear back to Russia!"

Simcha almost dropped the kugel.

"It's a miracle!" he declared. "Boruch Hashem!"

"No more worries about being

drafted into the Russian army, eh, Simcha?" asked Ephraim with a smile.

"No Jew was safe with those Cossacks around," answered Simcha. He looked up at the heavens in silent thankfulness.

There was admiration on every face as Simcha made his rounds through the marketplace. The tailor and his wife, Leah, nodded their approval as he passed. The men pressed him for details of his adventure, and he lingered long after every last piece of kugel was sold.

Simcha returned home that night with a quick step and a light heart. He sat down to write a long letter to Papa, telling how Hashem had answered his prayers and saved him from the fearful Cossacks.

"Don't worry, dear Papa," he concluded. Hashem will surely continue to protect us and bring us all together again — safe and sound.

"Your loving son, Simcha Bunim Nelkenbaum."

Chapter Seven

Papa's Letter

As the weeks went by, Simcha's confidence grew. Although the Jewish ghetto saw little improvement under the Germans, Simcha's fear of being drafted had disappeared. He walked easily through the streets to the marketplace each day.

One day Mama said, "Simcha, with all our hard work, I've been able to save enough money to start a new business. What would you think if we opened a small grocery store nearby?"

"That would be wonderful, Mama," he said.

"And a lot easier on our fingers," said

Suri, holding up her red, blistered hands. Everyone laughed. Now that they had an income, they could afford a sense of humor again.

Mama and Simcha looked for a suitable location for their store, but the only place they could afford was in a bad part of town. Gangs, thieves and other riff-raff wandered the streets.

"I don't like it, Mama," said Simcha. "It isn't safe."

"Nothing is safe in this Golus, Simcha. I won't let my daughters ruin their hands grating potatoes every night!"

"But Mama..."

"No buts, Simcha." Mama slashed the air with her arm, cutting off further discussion. "It's done."

Mama paid the landlord the first

month's rent. She and Simcha stocked the small store as best they could, given the shortage of goods.

Shmuel, the beggar boy, offered to help in the store. Simcha refused, but Shmuel's mother insisted.

"It's the least we can do after all your kindness. We wouldn't have made it through the winter without your help."

"Please, Simcha! I won't be any trouble, honest," Shmuel piped up.

Simcha saw the admiration glowing in Shmuel's eyes. He couldn't help being pleased.

"Alright," he said, pulling Shmuel's cap over his eyes. "We can always use more hands."

After several weeks, Simcha realized that all their customers treated them with respect. There was never any trouble. Shmuel told anyone who would listen about Simcha's struggle with the Cossacks. Each time he told the tale, it got bigger and bigger.

One day, an ill-tempered man with a scar across his nose requested some herring. As Mama nervously handed him the package, he nodded toward Simcha. "Is that the kid that flattened six Cossacks on his own?" Simcha turned red with embarrassment.

"Good work, kid." The man smiled, revealing a row of broken teeth.

Mama was speechless. When the man left the store, Mama looked at Simcha, then at Shmuel, then back at Simcha. Suddenly, they all burst out

laughing. They laughed until tears ran down their cheeks.

"Your reputation has earned us some respect around here," said Mama, wiping her eyes.

When they arrived home, Suri waved a letter at them. "It's from Papa, and it's addressed to Simcha!"

"To me?" asked Simcha. It was curious since all of Papa's other letters had been addressed to Mama.

Simcha's stomach churned as he opened the letter. He scanned it quickly and smiled.

"Read it to us!" cried Zisha.

Simcha cleared his throat. "To my dear son, Simcha Bunim. Boruch Hashem, you are safe. When Mama wrote about what happened, I thought you were foolish to fight with the Cossacks. I was angry that you would cause so much worry for your mother.

"Now that I received your letter, I understand that you were protecting the family, just as I asked you to. And so, dear son, I'm proud of you.

"I pray for this war to end, and hope that I may see you very soon. Until that time, I know that Mama and the children are in good hands.

"From your devoted father, Noyach Nelkenbaum."

Simcha stopped as if the letter ended there, but Papa had added one extra line at the bottom. "My dear son, I am sure that my yarmulke must fit you by now."

Simcha beamed with pride. He ran to get Papa's velvet yarmulke. With shaking hands, he carefully placed it on his head.

Somehow, without Simcha even noticing, it had become just the right size. Papa's yarmulke finally fit him!

Author's Note

In times of adversity, the sanctity and tradition of mitzvos bind the Jewish family together. Whether it is faithfully praying for Moshiach to come, or pretending to eat a full Shabbos dinner when only dry bread is available, the human spirit prevails.

The Great Potato Plan is based on true events in the history of my family. In 1910, my great-grandfather, Noyach (Nathan) Nelkenbaum, displayed that spirit when he left Poland to build a better life for his family in America.

His children and his wife, Ruchel (Rose), pregnant with their seventh child, stayed in Warsaw. Arriving through the port of Galveston, Texas, he took the last name Nelkin and settled in Kansas City.

One year later, he had only enough

money to bring one member of the family over the ocean. It was decided that the oldest child, Temela (Tillie), would go.

Another three years passed, and Noyach sent steamship tickets for the rest of the family. Two days before Ruchel and the six remaining children were to leave Poland, World War I broke out, delaying their departure for another seven years.

In the spring of 1920, the entire family was finally reunited in S. Joseph, Missouri where they gathered to celebrate Passover, the Festival of Freedom. The youngest child, Zisha (Cecil), was ten years old when he met his father for the first time.

When Simcha (Sam) and Hindel (Helen) grew up, they became engaged to be married. However, for five years after Simcha had come to America, his intended bride was not allowed through the tight immigration quotas.

Determined to keep his promise to marry her, Simcha returned to Warsaw in 1925. He married Hindel there and brought her to America as his wife. They had four children, including my father, Nedwyn.

Hindel continued a life-long friendship with Toba (Thelma) in Kansas City. She worked for many years as a saleswoman in Toba's clothing store.

I'm grateful to these generations past and appreciate the sacrifices they made. Without their courage and determination, I would not be here to tell their amazing story!

J.N.W.

Glossary

Glossary

Aleph-Bais - Hebrew alphabet.

Aron Kodesh - Holy ark in the synagogue that houses the Torah scrolls.

Bar Mitzvah - a boy's thirteenth birthday when he acquires the religious responsibilities of adulthood.

Becher - cup, usually silver, filled with wine and used to make kiddush on Shabbos.

Beis Hamikdosh - The Holy Temple in Jerusalem, destroyed in 70 c.e. by the Romans.

Besomim - spices used in the Havdallah service.

Birchas Hamazon - Grace after meals.

Brochah - blessing.

Boruch Hashem - Thank G-d.

Caftan - Long, black coat, worn by some male Jews on the Shabbos, usually made of silk and tied with a sash around the waist.

Challah - pl. challos - Braided Shabbos loaf of bread.

Cheder - Elementary religious school for learning Torah.

Cholent - Slow-cooking Sabbath stew of meat and vegetables.

Cossack - Member of a group of people from southern Russia, famous as cavalrymen in the tzarist army.

Daven - Pray.

Droshky - pl. droshkies - Light, open Russian carriage.

Eichah - The Book of Lamentations, part of the third section of the Hebrew Bible, which recounts the destruction of the Temple in Jerusalem in poetical form.

Gefilte fish - Stewed fish balls.

Golus - Exile; Jewish dispersion after the destruction of the Temple in Jerusalem, especially referring to lands where Jews were persecuted and treated as undesirable strangers.

Hamotzi - Blessing over bread.

Hashem - G-d.

Havdallah - Ceremony on Saturday evening that marks the end of the Sabbath.

Kanal - Sewer system in Warsaw, fed by the Vistula River.

Kasha - Mush made from buckwheat groats.

Kiddush - Blessing over a cup of wine consecrating the Shabbos or other holiday.

Kinder - Children.

Knippl - Knot in a handkerchief to hold coins, used as a purse.

Kreplach - Dough filled with meat and boiled.

Kugel - Pudding made from potatoes, noodles or bread.

Minyan - Group of ten Jewish men necessary for public religious services.

Mitzvah - pl. mitzvos - A good deed, one of the 613 commandments.

Moshiach - Messiah.

Negel Vasser - Traditional washing of the hands upon awakening

Oy gevald/Oy vey - Oh, woe! Dear me!

Pogrom - Riot; organized mass murder of the local Jewish population, often initiated by the government.

Shabbos - Sabbath: day of rest.

Shema - the 'Hear O Israel' Prayer.

Shul - Synagogue.

Tefillin - phylacteries; leather boxes containing verses from the Torah bound to the head and arm with leather straps during weekday morning prayers.

Tishah B'Av - The ninth day of the month of Av, a fast day to remember the destruction of the Temple in Jerusalem.

Torah - The Five Books of Moses. Also refers to the entire body of Jewish wisdom, laws and teachings.

Tzar - Emperor or king; ruler of Russia.

Tzedakah - Charity.

Tzimmes - A side dish in which vegetables, dried fruit and sometimes meat are baked together.

Yarmulke - Skullcap worn by Jewish males at all times as a reminder that Hashem is above us all.

Yerushalayim - Jerusalem.

Yiddish - Language spoken by Jewish population in Eastern Europe

Zmiros - traditional Shabbos songs.

❧ ❧ ❧